Max
the Movie Director

by Trina Wiebe

Illustrations by
Helen Flook

Lobster Press ™

Max the Movie Director
Text © 2003 Trina Wiebe
Illustrations © 2003 Helen Flook

Published by Lobster Press™
1620 Sherbrooke Street West, Suites C & D
Montréal, Québec   H3H 1C9
Tel. (514) 904-1100 • Fax (514) 904-1101 • www.lobsterpress.com

Publisher: Alison Fripp
Editor: Kathryn Cole
Graphic Production: Tammy Desnoyers

Distributed in the United States by:
Publishers Group West
1700 Fourth Street
Berkeley, CA 94710

Distributed in Canada by:
Raincoast Books
9050 Shaughnessey Street
Vancouver, BC V6P 6E5

We acknowledge the financial support of the Government of Canada through the Book
Publishing Industry Development Program (BPIDP) for our publishing activities.

The Canada Council | Le Conseil des Arts
for the Arts | du Canada

We acknowledge the support of the Canada
Council for the Arts for our publishing program.

National Library of Canada Cataloguing in Publication Data
Wiebe, Trina, 1970-
      Max the movie director / Trina Wiebe, author ; Kathryn Cole, editor ;
Helen Flook, illustrator.

(Max-a-million, ISSN 1701-4557 ; 3)
ISBN 1-894222-69-5

I. Cole, Kathryn II. Flook, Helen III. Title. IV. Series:Wiebe, Trina, 1970-   .
Max-a-million ; 3.

PS8595.I358M395 2003   jC813'.6   C2002-903954-1
PZ7

Printed and bound in Canada

Table of Contents

① The Buzzing Brain

"Did you see the slime?" cried Max, his eyes wide with excitement. "It shot right out of his nose!"

"Yeah," said Sid, munching popcorn. "Very cool."

"*Space Crusaders* is my favorite movie," Max declared. He stepped out of the dark theater into the afternoon sunshine. "It has everything. Spaceships and lasers and time portals and aliens . . . don't you just love it?"

Sid tilted her popcorn box and let the last buttery pieces roll into her mouth. "Uh huh."

"Wanna see it again?" Max asked.

Sid groaned and tossed the popcorn box into a nearby trash can. "Forget it," she said. "Five times in two weeks is my limit."

"But it's the greatest movie ever made," said Max. He pointed at the glossy movie poster hanging in the theater window. "It says so right there."

"Yeah, yeah," said Sid without looking.

"It's a huge box office hit," added Max. "It grossed over twenty million dollars during its opening . . ."

". . . weekend," finished Sid. "I know. You've mentioned that a hundred times, already."

"Well, it's true," said Max. He stared wistfully at the movie poster. A drooling three-headed alien stared back at him. Twenty million dollars. In one weekend! The words were like music to his ears.

Max had always known he was meant to be rich. It was his destiny. Someone with a name like Maximillian J. Wigglesworth III was supposed to have so much money that he'd need to hire a dozen people to count it, and another dozen to help him carry it. If only he could come up with the perfect money-making plan.

"I don't care if it grossed a hundred million dollars, I'm tired of watching it," said Sid. She grabbed the brim of the Brooksville Batters cap that she always wore and turned it around backwards on her head. "Wanna hang out at your house?"

Max looked at the movie poster once more, then shrugged and followed Sid down the street. "Fine," he grumbled. "But I'm coming back for the Sunday matinee."

They walked together in comfortable silence. After being best friends for three years, they didn't always need to talk. Max glanced at Sid. Her real name was Serendipity Sunshine

Stubberfield, although she'd die of embarrassment if anyone ever found out.

He watched her toss a stick of gum into her mouth and chew it noisily, popping and cracking it between her teeth. She blew a small bubble, then sucked it back into her mouth and bit it in half.

"What are you looking at?" she asked, noticing Max's gaze.

Max didn't answer. He was getting that familiar tingly feeling in his brain, the one he got when a particularly good idea came to him.

He squinted at Sid from a different angle. He noticed the way the light bounced off her favorite shirt, a worn baseball jersey with a faded number eleven on the back. And her messy orange curls made an interesting contrast with her freckled face.

"Quit staring," said Sid. She swiped the back of her hand over her chin. "Have I got butter on my face or something?"

Max stopped suddenly and held up both hands, palm out. He closed one eye and framed Sid between his thumbs and forefingers. "Wait," he said. "Hold it right there."

Sid froze. "What's wrong?" she asked from between clenched teeth. "Is there a wasp on me?"

Max grinned. His brain was buzzing full blast now. "Nope," he said, circling around Sid, still viewing her through his hands. "You have great cheekbones, you know."

Sid snorted. "Have you lost your mind?"

"No," said Max with a laugh. "But I think I've just found the perfect money-making idea!"

Sid groaned and started walking. "Here we go again."

Max hurried to catch up. "No, wait, Sid. I'm serious. This time my plan will really work!"

"I've heard that before," she said without slowing down. "Don't tell me, let me guess. You're going to be a space crusader, right? You're going to build a spaceship and travel throughout the universe like the guy in the movie, searching for priceless space crystals. Oh, and you want me to be your copilot. Am I close?"

"No," grumbled Max. He shoved his hands in his pockets. "That's just silly."

Sid stopped and faced Max. "Of course it's silly. All your ideas are silly. Like last time, when you decided to be a superhero."

"We saved those puppies," Max reminded her.

"Yeah," agreed Sid. "But we didn't get rich, did we?"

Max waved away her question. "No, but this new idea is a real winner. It can't fail!"

Sid put her hands over her ears. "I don't want to hear this."

"But it's perfect," cried Max. He had that zany, unfocused look in his eyes, like he was seeing things that nobody else could see. "It's amazing. It's marvelous. It's absolutely the best idea I've ever had!"

Sid sighed and let her hands drop. "What is it?"

Max thumped his chest dramatically with one hand. "I, Maximillian J. Wigglesworth III, am going to direct a blockbuster movie," he announced with a grin. "And you, Dippy, are going to be my star!"

2 Into Production

"A movie?" repeated Sid, her mouth hanging open.

"A blockbuster movie," corrected Max.

Sid blinked several times. "And I'm the star?"

"Yes, of course," cried Max. He put both hands on Sid's cheeks and squeezed until her lips puckered like a trout. "Soon, everyone will know this face. You're going to be famous. And I'm going to be rich!"

Sid shook off Max's hands. She scowled and rubbed her cheeks. "I'm not an actor," she objected. "And you're not a director. You don't even have a camera."

"Maybe not yet," said Max, grabbing her by the elbow and tugging her forward. "But I know where to get one."

Sid was still protesting when Max dragged her through the front gate and up the path to his house.

"Hi, Mom," said Max, spotting the soles of her gardening clogs under a leafy shrub.

Mom poked her head up through the greenery. "Hi, kids. How was the movie?"

"Outstanding," gushed Max. "Absolutely, totally, and completely fantabulistic!"

"That's quite a review," smiled Mom. She flicked a ladybug off of one shoulder with a gloved finger. "I'm glad you had fun."

"Is Dad around?" asked Max.

"I saw him a few minutes ago," said Mom, pointing at the house. "He was just finishing breakfast."

"Breakfast was hours ago," said Max. He noticed Mom's prize-winning delphiniums were meticulously weeded and watered. She always lost track of time when she was working in her flower garden.

"It was?" Mom wrinkled her forehead. "I'd better hop into the shower or I'll be late for work."

"A tardy librarian," giggled Max, heading up the porch steps. "Maybe you'll have to pay a late fine."

The kitchen was empty and the breakfast dishes were washed and put away. Max led Sid through the living room, also empty, and down the hall to Dad's den. He knocked lightly, then pushed the door open.

"Anybody home?" he asked, stepping inside.

Dad glanced up from the computer. "I'll be with you in a minute."

Max grimaced at Sid, who rolled her eyes toward the ceiling. They both knew that when it came to Mr. and Mrs. Wigglesworth, a minute could turn into a month. Max's parents didn't ignore him on purpose. They were very kind and loving – once you caught their attention.

"Dad, could you do me a favor?" asked Max.

"Hold on," Dad said, crouched over the keyboard. The computer pinged and bleeped. "I just have to finish this paragraph . . ."

Max sighed. Then he spotted something on a shelf beside the desk, and brightened. He walked across the room and ran his fingertips over Dad's newest toy, a portable video camera that fit in the palm of his hand. Its shiny knobs and buttons gleamed invitingly.

"Can I borrow this?" Max asked.

"Um hmmm..." mumbled Dad, typing furiously.

With a grin, Max picked up the tiny camera. Sometimes having parents who only half paid attention to you came in handy. "Thanks, Dad. I'll be super careful."

He was nearly out the door when the clacking of computer keys abruptly stopped.

"Max?" asked Dad. "Where do you think you're going with that?"

Max slowly turned around. He held up the camera. "You mean this?"

Dad nodded.

"Well," began Max. "Sid and I . . ."

Sid, who was still lurking in the doorway, groaned and shook her head.

"*I*," continued Max, "have decided to make a movie. I'm going to film it, and Sid is going to be my star. I just need to borrow your video camera to get it all on tape. Or, in the can, as they say in the biz."

"I see," said Dad. "And you probably plan on selling your movie to Hollywood and making a million dollars . . ."

"Twenty million, actually," corrected Max.

Dad raised his eyebrows, but continued talking. ". . . however, I'm not sure I'm willing to let you run around with my brand new camera. It's very expensive and we had to save up a long time to buy it. If you wait until I'm finished here, maybe I could help."

"But you bought the camera three weeks ago," complained Max, "and you haven't even touched it."

"I know, Max," said Dad with a shrug. "I've

had several big articles to finish lately, and I'm writing a weekly column for the newspaper now . . ."

"Exactly," said Max. "You're always too busy. If I have to wait for you I'll never start my movie, let alone finish it."

Dad looked at the work piled beside his computer and sighed. "True."

"So please, please can I borrow it?" begged Max. *"Please?"*

"Well . . ." said Dad slowly, staring at the camera. "Okay. But be careful. Someday I plan on having some free time and I'd like to be able to video tape it."

"It's safe with me," promised Max. "And don't worry, I'll include your name as co-producer in the closing credits."

Dad sighed. "Great."

Max cradled the camera against his chest and hurried from the room before Dad could change his mind. His plan was working perfectly. He had a camera, a leading lady, and the brilliant creative mind needed to shoot a box office smash hit.

It was time to make movie magic.

3 Your Name in Lights

"We're rolling," called Max, peering through the camera's viewfinder.

Sid gulped. "L-line?"

Max hit the pause button and sighed. "For the last time, you don't have any lines in this scene. You're an ordinary girl who stumbles onto a space-ship in the woods, gets captured by aliens, then escapes just in time to save Earth from total annihilation. It's so simple. Now get on your bike and ride toward me. And don't forget to smile."

"Okay," said Sid. She took a deep breath. "I'll get it right this time."

"Good," said Max. He lifted the camera to his eye. "Scene one, take seven. And . . . action!"

Smiling woodenly at the camera, Sid climbed on her bike and pedaled across the front yard toward Max. The kickstand, still lowered, dragged behind her. It cut a jagged brown line into the lawn. A blob of grass and leaves collected on the end of it, but Sid kept pedaling.

"You're doing great," encouraged Max, following her with the camera. "Beautiful, Sid. Just marvelous."

Sid kept her lips pulled back from her teeth in a determined grin and pedaled harder. For once she wasn't wearing a baseball cap, and her hair blew in the wind. She didn't look away from the camera even when her front tire rolled over a garden hose.

"Keep coming," said Max, the camera focused on her face.

The hose snagged on the kickstand and the bike jerked to a stop. Sid, however, kept on going. She sailed over the handlebars, teeth bared, straight at Max.

Crash!

Sid barreled into Max like a linebacker in a football game and they crumpled to the ground. Max lay flat on his back, stunned, the camera clutched in both hands.

"Cut," he croaked.

"Sorry," gasped Sid. She rolled off him and climbed unsteadily to her feet. A red welt spread across her forehead. "I told you I can't act."

"Are you kidding?" cried Max. He checked the camera. The green light blinked at him. "That was great! I got the whole thing on tape. Let's shoot the next scene."

Sid groaned. "The next scene?"

Max scrambled to his feet. "Yeah, the one where you stumble onto the abandoned spaceship. Only it's not abandoned, and the aliens chase you through the woods. I'm going to start from far away, then zoom in for a close-up. I want real emotions, Sid. Give me surprise, then disbelief, then terror..."

"That sounds hard," said Sid. "How are you going to zoom through the forest without tripping? And where are we going to get a spaceship? Or a forest for that matter?"

Max paused. "Good point."

"I think we need help," said Sid. "Maybe we *should* wait for your dad . . ."

"Nah," said Max. "He's too busy. So is Mom. Besides, I'm in charge here and I need somebody I can give orders to. Someone who will obey my every command, who will run and fetch without question..."

Max and Sid looked at each other. "The Thompson sisters!"

The Thompson sisters, Cora and Ivy, lived two doors down from the Wigglesworths. They used to follow Max like faithful puppies until last summer, when he accidentally set their clothesline ablaze with his homemade fire baton. He hadn't seen them much after that.

"Do you think they'll help?" asked Sid.

"Of course they will," said Max. He smiled confidently and patted the camera. "Who can possibly resist the chance to see their name up in lights?"

4 That Star Quality

"No way," said Cora.

"But . . ." began Max.

"Not in a million, billion years." Cora crossed her arms over her chest and glowered at Max from under a blonde fringe of hair. "Not after what happened last time."

"That wasn't my fault," protested Max. He turned to Ivy for help. "You believe me, don't you?"

Ivy smiled shyly and nodded. "Please, Cora," she said to her sister. "Your eyebrows grew back a long time ago. And making a movie sounds like fun."

"Sounds like trouble to me," snapped Cora.

Ivy clasped her hands together under her chin and stared imploringly at Cora. "Pretty please?"

"I'll put your names in the credits,"

promised Max.

Cora sniffed.

"Maybe I can use you as extras in the movie," Max added. "Wouldn't you like to see yourself on the silver screen?"

"No," said Cora.

"Oh, yes!" cried Ivy. She grabbed Cora and pulled her aside, but Max could still hear what they were saying.

"If we can help Max with his movie," Ivy whispered, "I won't tell Daddy you failed your last spelling test."

Cora's cheeks flushed pink. "You swore you wouldn't tattle. That's blackmail."

Ivy smiled.

Cora scowled. "Fine."

Ivy turned back to Max. "Where do we start?" she asked.

Max clapped his hands together. "We'll shoot the next scene at my house. We can pretend Mom's garden is a forest. Ivy, we need tinfoil, lots of it – and makeup. Sid, practice looking scared. Oh, and Cora, be a sweetheart and get me a drink. Lemonade. Extra sugar, no ice."

Cora opened her mouth, but Ivy shot her a warning look, so she snapped it shut again and stomped off without a word.

Fifteen minutes later they met in the Wigglesworths' backyard. Max sported the Scottish tam Dad wore when he played bagpipes in the local marching band. It was tilted on his head at a jaunty angle. A red sweater was knotted about his shoulders, completing the outfit.

Max clapped his hands loudly. "People, people, please! We're losing the light."

Sid rolled her eyes. "We're right here."

"Excellent," said Max briskly. He rattled off instructions for the next scene, including the construction of a tinfoil spaceship, then thrust something at Sid. "Here. Put this on."

Sid stared at it. It was one of Mrs. Wigglesworth's old dresses, pink and green and flowery. "Why?"

"Because," said Max, rolling his eyes

skyward, "Your character is coming home from a school dance when she finds the spaceship, remember?"

"It looks awfully big," said Sid. "Besides, you know I hate dresses."

Max ignored her and turned to Ivy and Cora. "Places everyone," he yelled in their faces. "Let's get this show on the road."

"We're not deaf," grumbled Cora, bending over to grab the handle of a little red wagon.

"Take a moment to really get into your character's head," Max urged Sid as he watched her struggle into the dress. Ivy hovered nearby, frantically dabbing powder on Sid's bruised forehead. "Find her motivation. Feel her emotions. Remember . . . I want panic. Fear. Terror."

Sid scowled, gathered up the long skirt with both arms, and stomped away to her place behind the tool shed.

Max grabbed the camera and climbed into the wagon. He lifted one hand in the air, paused dramatically, then yelled, "Cue sound, cue lights, cue actors . . . and action!"

Nothing happened.

"And . . . action!" Max shouted.

There was a thud, followed by a yelp, then Sid came into sight, riding her bike. She'd hitched the dress up around her waist and tucked part of it into her jeans, but the hem still trailed along the ground behind her.

Ivy stepped in front of the camera and smacked a pair of tap shoes together so that the soles made a sharp clapping noise. "Scene two, take one."

Sid rode toward Max, the dress flapping as she pedaled. Her lips were twisted in an odd, stiff grimace.

"Cue wagon," ordered Max.

"Cora," hissed Ivy.

"Oh, right," said Cora. She yanked on the wooden handle and the wagon, with Max in it, lurched forward. Ivy ran to help her sister, and the two of them dragged the wagon across the lawn, staying ahead of Sid so that Max could get the perfect shot.

"More terror," directed Max, bracing his feet against the back edge of the wagon.

Sid stretched her lips wider.

"Come on, Sid," urged Max. "Show me some real fear."

Sid scowled, then suddenly her eyes went round and her jaw dropped open.

"Marvelous," cried Max.

"Help," cried Sid. Her shoulders hunched lower and lower until her chin nearly touched the handlebars.

"That's right," said Max. "Improvise!"

"My dress," gurgled Sid. The hem of the dress was twisted around her foot, winding tighter and tighter with each turn of the pedal.

Riiiiiip!

The hem tore free and the skirt flew upward, flapping crazily in Sid's face. Blinded, Sid let go of the handlebars, and the bike swerved sharply to the left.

"Ahhhhh," screamed Sid.

"Ahhhhhhhhhh," screamed Cora and Ivy in unison.

"Wonderful," yelled Max, recording it all.

Sid clawed at the shredded material, then grabbed for the handlebars, but it was too late. The bike smashed into a garden gnome, knocking it over and shattering its pointy ears. Frantically, Sid jerked the handlebars to the right, sideswiping a wheelbarrow full of weeds. Shrieking at the top of her lungs, Sid veered through a bed of daisies, heading straight for a large mound of garden soil that had been delivered the day before. The bike ploughed into the soft dirt and Sid landed on top of it like a cherry on an ice-cream sundae.

"That was beautiful, Sid," cried Max.

"Simply brilliant!" He jumped out of the wagon and ran over to her. "But could you do it again, this time with a little more energy?"

5 A Suspicious Caller

Sid spat out a mouthful of dirt. "Do it again?" she repeated.

"Yeah," cried Max. "And after that, I want to shoot the scene where you're sucked into the spaceship by an invisible force field. Ivy and Cora can climb a tree and we'll tie ropes under your arms and . . ."

"I quit," said Sid.

Max stopped talking and stared. "You what?"

"I quit," Sid repeated. She stood up and calmly shook the soil out of her hair. Then she stepped out of the stained and torn dress, and strode away. "Find another leading lady," she called over her shoulder, "because I'm out of here."

"Wait," cried Max, losing his tam as he scurried after her. "You were great! The emotion on your face was . . ."

Sid whirled around. "You want emotion? Well here's some emotion for you. I've got dirt up my nose and my bike is ruined and I'm very, very sore!" she yelled. "How's that for emotion?"

Max stared at her. "But you can't quit. I need you. Without you, there is no movie."

Sid took a deep breath. "Sorry, Max. I'm no good at this acting stuff. Besides," she added. "My bike is toast."

Max looked at Sid's bike. Bits of frayed fabric stuck out from the pedal and chain, and the front wheel was bent. It looked bad.

Ivy patted Sid's arm. "Don't worry about your bike, Sid. My daddy can fix anything. One time Cora left her bike in the driveway and . . ."

"Never mind that," said Cora. She frowned at Ivy and grabbed Sid's bike by the handlebars. "Let's just take this to the shop."

Max grinned. "Problem solved."

Ivy grabbed Max's tam and Max and Cora dragged Sid's bike all the way to Main Street. Sid walked silently beside them, shaking dirt out of her clothes. When they reached the bike shop,

Ivy held the door open and Max and Cora carried the mangled bicycle inside.

"Daddy?" called Cora. "Are you here?"

A slim, balding man stepped out of an office at the rear of the store. "Hi kids, what have you got there?"

Max glanced at Sid. "We kind of had a stunt accident," he said. "A minor production glitch, really."

Sid snorted.

"I promised you'd fix it," said Ivy.

Mr. Thompson looked at the wreckage. "Good grief. I certainly hope someone was wearing a helmet."

Sid glared at Max.

"Daddy likes to talk about bike safety," said Cora, rolling her eyes. "It's his favorite subject."

Mr. Thompson wagged his finger at Cora. "Bike safety is extremely important. Did you know that non-helmeted bike riders are fourteen times more likely to be involved in a fatal crash than helmeted riders? Research shows that wearing a helmet can reduce the risk of head injury by as much as 85 percent. In fact, last year alone there were . . ."

"I know, Daddy," interrupted Cora. "I was at your last bike safety seminar, remember?" She dragged the bike closer. "Can you fix it?"

Mr. Thompson picked up the bike and carried it to a workbench. He fitted it into a large metal brace and studied it for a moment. "Yes," he finally said. "It'll be as good as new when I'm finished."

Ivy and Cora hugged him. "Thanks, Daddy," they said together.

Mr. Thompson smiled down at his daughters. Then he glanced at his watch. Worry lines creased his forehead. "Well, kids, I'm just closing up. I'll have to work on the bike another time. I've got a meeting now."

"But we need the bike to finish the movie," protested Ivy.

Mr. Thompson shook his head. "Sorry, sweetie. I've got an appointment with Mr. Sherman."

Max watched Cora and Ivy exchange a glance. Then the front door of the store opened and a man with a bushy brown moustache walked in. Or rather, limped in. He was on crutches, one leg in a cast up to his knee. A thick white brace wrapped around his neck and a large bandage covered most of his forehead.

"You kids run along," said Mr. Thompson in a strained voice. He shooed them out the door. "You can pick up the bike in a few days."

"Thanks, Mr. Thompson," said Sid, but the door had already slammed shut.

6 Twisting the Plot

"Who was that guy?" asked Max, standing on the sidewalk in front of the bike shop. "He looks like he jumped out of an airplane, but forgot to pack his parachute."

"Maybe he's starring in a movie, too," joked Sid. Max grinned. He knew Sid couldn't stay mad at him for long.

"That was Willy Sherman," said Cora. She stuck her tongue out at the shop window. "He's a big, fat liar."

"Why?" asked Max.

Ivy answered for her. "We heard Daddy talking to Mommy last night," she said. "Mr. Sherman was in an accident. He says there was something wrong with the bicycle he bought from Daddy."

Cora stomped her foot. "He's lying. You heard Daddy back there. He's a safety freak. He triple-checks every single one of his bikes. Mr. Sherman's accident wasn't Daddy's fault."

"Maybe he's going to sue your dad," said Max.

He'd seen enough small claims court on television to recognize a potential lawsuit when he saw one.

"I think he's faking it," said Ivy. She grabbed her sister's arm. "Just like that time you didn't want to go to school and you put the thermometer on the lamp and Mom thought you had a fever and . . ."

"You're such a blabbermouth!" cried Cora. She twisted free of Ivy's grip. "Why do you have to be such a tattletale?"

"Maybe we should go back to Max's house now," Sid said, trying to distract the arguing sisters. "We should probably work on that spaceship, since we can't shoot the rest of the movie for a while. Right, Max?"

Max stared at the bike shop. His eyes were unfocused and he wore a strange grin on his face, one that was slowly growing bigger and bigger. If Mr. Sherman sued Mr. Thompson, they'd have to go to court. Maybe they'd even get in the newspaper. Everybody loved to gossip about an interesting court case.

"Max?" repeated Sid, louder.

"What's wrong with him?" whispered Ivy.

"Nothing," sighed Sid. She had seen this look many times before and it always spelled trouble, with a capital T. "He's just . . ."

"I've got a brilliant idea," cried Max. Television was filled with all kinds of law shows. Real courts with real judges, and fictional courts with pretend lawyers and prosecutors and defendants. The viewing audience was fascinated by it.

Sid gingerly rubbed her forehead. "I hope it doesn't involve ladders, ropes, or a tall tree."

Cora touched her eyebrows. "Or fire."

"No, no, no," said Max. He spun in a circle and hurled his tam into the air. His brain whirled at supersonic speed. "Forget the aliens and the spaceship and the invisible force field. Forget it all!"

Ivy inched closer to Sid. "We're not making a movie anymore?"

Max scooped up the fallen tam and plunked it back on his head. "Oh, we're making a movie all right," he said. "Just not a space alien one. That's been done already. I want to do something fresh, something important."

"Like what?" asked Sid suspiciously.

Max grinned. "Courtroom drama."

Sid thought about that for a moment. "No more crazy bike stunts?"

"Nope," said Max.

"No more floppy dresses or phony emotions?" she asked, just to make sure.

"Nope," answered Max. "From now on, you're a girl who has witnessed illegal dumping of toxic sludge and you're going to single-handedly take a huge chemical industry to court and make them pay billions of dollars to clean up the pollution."

Sid looked skeptical. "That doesn't sound very realistic, Max."

"It's classic," insisted Max. "The little guy takes on the powerful giant. The underdog fights back. You hear about it in the news all the time."

"But I'm just a kid," said Sid.

Max nodded eagerly. "That's what makes it special. Trust me, the audience will eat it up with a spoon. Let's go, guys. We're wasting precious production time."

7 Movie Magic

"Where exactly are we going?" asked Sid.

Max jogged down the street with Cora and Ivy hot on his heels. "To the library, of course," he called over his shoulder. "Where else would a girl fighting a mega-corporation research the law?"

Sid shrugged and ran to catch up with them. Soon they were climbing the steep stone steps of the Brooksville Public Library.

"Luckily, the library's open late tonight. We have time to shoot the scene where you dig up dirt on the chemical company," explained Max. "I want you up to your eyebrows in big fat law books, researching, reading, looking for evidence."

"Sounds pretty safe," said Sid. "I think I'm going to like this movie."

Max held the door open for Ivy and Cora. "Later I'll add music. You know, the kind they play to show time passing. You won't have to say a thing."

"Perfect," grinned Sid. "I can never remember my lines anyway."

They made their way past the children's area to the reference section. There they were surrounded by floor-to-ceiling bookshelves containing thick, leather-bound volumes. Max headed straight for the encyclopedias.

"These could look like law books," he said, selecting several at random. "Let's spread them all over the table to make it seem like Sid has been working for hours."

"They're heavy," grunted Ivy, pulling volumes *A* through *D* off the shelf.

Cora grabbed volumes *E* and *F* before they hit the floor. "Watch it, Ivy," she snapped, "or I'll be in a cast just like Mr. Sherman."

"This looks good," interrupted Max. He plunked a tall stack of books on the table beside one of the library's public computers. "Okay, people. Let's get this scene in the bag."

Sid sat in the chair in front of the computer. She chose an encyclopedia and opened it, pretending to be completely absorbed. "How's this?" she asked out of the corner of her mouth.

Max pulled out the camera and turned it on. He focused on Sid's hunched figure. "Perfect," he said. "Now flip some pages."

Sid turned a page, pretended to read, then turned a few more. Getting into her character, she leaned forward and typed something on the computer keyboard.

"Great," said Max. "Now act like you're taking notes or something."

Sid was having fun. She ran her finger down a line of text and paused, like she'd just discovered something important. Leaning forward, she stretched her arm toward a pad of paper. Her elbow accidentally knocked the tall stack of encyclopedias.

"Watch out!" cried Cora.

Sid jerked her elbow back, but the tower of books teetered, toppled over, and crashed into a half-empty book return cart. The cart lurched forward on the smooth floor and rolled in the direction of the reception desk.

Mrs. Wigglesworth, her arms filled with

magazines, screamed and leaped out of the way as the runaway cart zoomed toward her. It slammed into a freestanding bookrack filled with paperback romance novels, which knocked over a rack of westerns. In an awful chain reaction, the westerns sent a rack of detective stories flying. When the last book hit the floor, a shocked silence fell over the library.

Sid gulped. "Oops."

Mrs. Wigglesworth ran over. "What on earth is going on here?" she demanded.

"I'm making a movie," said Max.

"Your father mentioned that," said Mom. Her gaze fell on the camera and she frowned. "What he failed to tell me was that you were going to shoot it here. In my nice, quiet library."

"Don't worry about the mess, Mrs. Wigglesworth," said Cora. "We'll clean it up."

"Yeah," added Sid. "I'm really sorry. Every time Max turns that thing on, I become a total klutz. It's like I'm cursed or something." She bent over to pick up the encyclopedias scattered around their feet, but her shoulder caught the edge of the table. The computer monitor trembled.

"Leave it!" cried Mom, steadying the table with both hands. "Please, we'll take care of the mess. You kids go somewhere else to destroy, er, I mean film your movie."

"Are you sure?" asked Max.

Mom shooed them toward the door. "I'm positive. Take your film on location. Anywhere but here!"

8   Background Information

Max sat on the bottom library step and stared at the camera thoughtfully. "Making a movie is a lot harder than I thought," he said.

"So, what's next?" asked Ivy, plopping down beside him.

Max fiddled with the camera buttons. The camera whirred in his hands as it rewound.

"Maybe we should watch the rushes now."

"Watch the who?" asked Sid.

"The rushes," explained Max, squinting at the tiny view screen, "are the things you've already filmed."

Ivy, Cora, and Sid crowded close as Max hit the "play" button. They leaned forward and watched Sid pedal onscreen.

"That's funny," giggled Ivy, as Sid tangled with the garden hose.

"It gets better," said Max with a grin.

"So that's how you got that bruise," snickered Cora as the miniature Sid flew over her handlebars.

"Do we have to watch this?" grumbled Sid. "I thought the space alien movie was history."

"I guess you're right," said Max. He fast-forwarded through the rest of Sid's bicycle scenes until he reached the library footage. A tiny Sid sat in front of a tiny computer, engrossed in her research. "Here we go."

Sid turned away. "I can't watch."

Ivy giggled again. "There goes the book cart!"

"Wow," said Cora, "I didn't know librarians could jump so high. This is great, Max. You should be making a comedy, not a courtroom drama."

Max stared at Cora thoughtfully. "A comedy?" he repeated. Everyone liked to laugh. Comedians made movies all the time. "Hey, maybe you're onto something there," he said. "Why let all this great footage go to waste? Sid could be this kid who is totally accident prone and . . ."

"Hey, look," interrupted Ivy. "It's Mr. Sherman."

Max glanced up the street, but Ivy was pointing at the viewing screen. She leaned forward and hit the pause button.

"It really is him," she said. "There, in the background." Sure enough, Willy Sherman was on the video, standing in a group of shocked onlookers.

"What's he doing in the library?" asked Ivy. "I thought he was meeting with Daddy."

"I guess it didn't take long," said Cora. She looked glum.

"Wait a second," said Max. He rewound the tape, then played it again. Something wasn't right. Max watched Sid knock the stack of encyclopedias into the book cart again, studying Mr. Sherman in the background. Just like the people on both sides of him, Mr. Sherman instinctively twisted his neck to watch the disastrous domino effect.

"I don't believe it," whispered Max. He rewound the tape a third time.

"What is it?" asked Sid.

"Watch Mr. Sherman," said Max. He hit play.

"He's just standing there," complained Cora. "What's so exciting about that?"

"Keep watching," said Max. "See what he does when Sid knocks the books over?"

"He does the same thing everyone else does," said Cora. "Stare. The crash was so loud everyone in the whole library heard it."

"Exactly," said Max. "The noise was loud and unexpected and everyone turned to see what was happening. Including Willy Sherman."

"Except he's in a neck brace," said Sid. She looked up at Max, her eyes wide. "He shouldn't have been able to move his neck like that. He really is faking!"

"That's right," grinned Max, "And I have it all on tape."

9 Imposter in Plaster

"We have to show this tape to Daddy," cried Cora, jumping to her feet. "It'll solve all his problems."

Max rewound the tape to the beginning of Sid's library scene so it would be ready to show to Mr. Thompson, or maybe even the police. Max was sure Officer Todd, a police officer who had helped Max in the past, would be extremely interested in this information.

"It's all set," said Max with a grin. "I just have to press play . . ."

He broke off, mid-sentence. Above them, the library door squeaked open.

"Someone's coming," hissed Sid.

"Hide," whispered Max. The library had two large stone lions standing guard at the bottom of the steps. Max ducked behind one lion. Sid, Cora and Ivy did the same on the other side.

Clump, scrape. Clump, scrape.

Trembling, Max peered around the lion's muzzle. He watched Mr. Sherman descend the steep stairs on his crutches. Thinking fast, Max whipped the camera up to his eye and trained it on Mr. Sherman. Maybe he'd get some more incriminating evidence.

But Mr. Sherman was being careful. Even though the street appeared deserted, he took his time, carefully placing the rubber tips of his crutches on each step. Max continued to film, wishing Mr. Sherman would slip up again.

At the bottom of the stairs he paused. Max expected him to catch his breath and continue down the street, but he simply stood there, like he was waiting for a bus or something. The longer Mr. Sherman stood there, the longer Max taped him.

Then, just when Max's arm was starting to ache, he heard another sound. This time it was the sharp clacking of high heels against concrete. A woman in a blue pinstripe suit walked up and stopped a few feet away.

"I don't like meeting like this," she snapped, staring straight ahead.

Mr. Sherman grunted and leaned on his crutches. "Why not? There's no law against two strangers talking on the street. Any news?"

"Nothing yet," she said, without looking at him. "But don't worry. Once he reads the letter I mailed yesterday, Mr. Thompson will be more than ready to settle. Nobody messes with Charlotte Tann."

Max sucked in his breath. He zoomed in on the pair. This was too good to be true!

Mr. Sherman snickered. "That's why you're the brains of this operation. Do you really think he'll fork over the money?"

Charlotte brushed a speck of lint off of her lapel. She stared into the air above Max's lion, her eyes flat and hard. "Oh, he'll settle all right."

"Let's celebrate," said Mr. Sherman. He leaned forward and captured Charlotte's hand in his own. "How about dinner and dancing? There's a new French restaurant a few towns over, nobody will be looking for us there. I'm in the mood for something expensive – deep-fried garlic snails and hot, buttered lobster tails – compliments of our good friend, Mr. Thompson."

Charlotte jerked her hand away. "Forget it. We don't have the money yet. If you blow this gig like you did in Harrington, we're through."

"But that wasn't my fault," began Mr. Sherman.

Charlotte gazed at him for the first time, fixing him with a look that was so chilly, even Max shivered. "Go back to the Blackberry Inn. Wait for my call. Understand?"

Mr. Sherman hung his head and nodded.

Without another word, she turned and stalked away. Mr. Sherman sighed and hobbled in the opposite direction.

"We've got them," crowed Max. He came out from behind the lion and held the camera in the air. "That was practically a confession, and I've got it all on tape! This is so perfect... forget space aliens or courtroom drama or even comedy. I'm making a hard-hitting documentary that will expose Mr. Sherman as a fraud. Your dad won't get sued and I'll have a prize-winning piece of investigative journalism!"

"What about that red light?" asked Sid.

Max stopped grinning. "What red light?"

"There," said Sid, pointing at the camera. She looked at Max and groaned. "Oh, don't tell me the battery ran out. You got the footage, right?"

"Of course," said Max. He inspected the camera closely. The green blinking light had definitely changed to red. How long had it been like that?

"Rewind it and check," said Sid.

Max played with the buttons, but nothing worked. "Oh, no," he muttered. "The batteries are completely dead."

10 The Harrington Connection

"So how's the movie coming?" asked Dad after a late supper that night. He scraped mashed potatoes into the garbage, then handed the plate to Max.

Max glumly stacked the plate in the dishwasher. Not only had the camera battery gone dead just before Charlotte arrived on the scene, but when Max got home and plugged the camera into an outlet, he discovered he'd accidentally taped over the library footage. Now all he had was five minutes of Mr. Sherman standing outside the library, waiting. The image of Mr. Sherman swiveling his "injured" neck didn't exist anymore. They were back to square one, with both the movie and helping Mr. Thompson.

"I dunno. Getting the perfect shot is harder than I thought," said Max.

"I know what you mean," said Dad. He

rinsed a handful of cutlery and passed it to Max. "It's just like writing a headline story for the newspaper. You want every word to be perfect, but sometimes you have to write three or four drafts before you get it right."

"I guess," said Max. Dad compared everything to his work as a reporter for the Brooksville Times.

"Take that article I wrote last month," continued Dad. "The one about those con artists over in Harrington. I must have written my opening paragraph ten times. I just couldn't find the perfect hook. The hook is what captures the reader's attention, you know," he explained. "You have to grab their interest right off the bat or they'll flip the page . . ."

"Did you say Harrington?" interrupted Max. The gears in his brain began to turn. Where had he heard that name before?

"That's right," nodded Dad, as he added dishwasher detergent to the full load of dirty dishes.

"What happened, again?" asked Max.

Dad paused, the soap still in his hand. "A man slipped near a public water fountain, pretended to hurt his back, and threatened to sue the town. He almost got away with it too, except someone twigged to the fact that he was lying."

"Who was he?" asked Max.

"He was some kind of dancer. A fellow by

the name of Sherman Windler, if I remember correctly," said Dad. "Apparently he used to be quite good. Musicals, television commercials, that sort of thing. Nowadays he makes his living conning people out of their money."

"So how come he's not in jail?" asked Max. He immediately thought of Willy Sherman. Sherman Windler. The names were eerily similar. And hadn't Mr. Sherman mentioned dancing?

Dad looked at Max curiously. "He always disappears before the police can arrest him. And he's hard to spot. Apparently, he learned a fair bit about stage makeup in the theater, because he never looks the same way twice. Why do you ask?"

Max shrugged and pretended to be interested in programming the rinse cycle. Could that bushy moustache be fake? "No reason," he said.

Dad didn't look convinced, but before he could question Max further, the phone rang.

"I'll get it," said Max. He left the kitchen,

answering on the extension in the living room.

"Hello?" he said.

"Max, it's Cora," said a trembling voice. "Everything is awful! Daddy is going to lose the store, we might have to sell our house and move and . . ."

"Calm down," instructed Max. "Tell me what happened."

"The letter came," said Cora. "Daddy is determined to pay Mr. Sherman off and settle out of court. Mommy is trying not to cry, and Ivy is hiding in her room."

Max frowned. "What else did your dad say?"

"I heard him say he was meeting with Mr. Sherman's lawyer at 10:00 a.m. tomorrow at the shop," sniffled Cora. "With his entire life savings. How are you going to catch Mr. Sherman before then?"

Max was wondering that himself. There was nothing they could do tonight. The camera battery wouldn't be fully charged yet. His brain whirled feverishly, trying to devise a plan that would expose Mr. Sherman for the trickster he was. Then, just like always, the perfect plan formed in his mind.

"Don't worry," he assured Cora. "I want you and Ivy to meet me behind the Blackberry Inn tomorrow morning at nine o'clock, sharp."

11 Plan of Action

Max pedaled as fast as he could without jarring the camera, which he'd tucked inside his shirt. He zipped up Main Street, past the bike shop with its "closed" sign hanging in the door, and down a back alley that brought him to the rear of the Blackberry Inn. As he got closer, he saw three figures huddled near the garbage cans.

"So what's the plan?" asked Sid without waiting for Max to get off his bike.

Max leaned it against a rickety fence and unsnapped his helmet. Then he pulled the video camera out and double-checked that the freshly charged battery was working.

"Same plan as before," he said, smiling reassuringly at Ivy and Cora. "We record him blowing his cover."

Cora put her hands on her hips and glared at Max. "That's it? Daddy is going to lose everything in exactly one hour, and you don't even have a new plan?"

"It'll work," said Ivy. Her eyes were swollen from crying. "Max won't let us down."

"It would have worked yesterday," said Max. "If the dumb battery hadn't run out." *And if I hadn't taped over the evidence*, he added silently.

"Don't worry," said Sid. She put her arm around Ivy. "We'll save your dad's bike shop."

"Right," said Max, slipping back into his role as director. Only this time he was directing a rescue mission, not a movie. "I called the hotel this morning. Mr. Sherman is in room eleven."

He paused to squint at the backside of the Blackberry Inn. It wasn't very big. He'd been inside it lots of times. He'd even stayed in room ten when Dad covered its 20th anniversary for the paper. He closed his eyes, remembering the layout. Then he opened them and carefully counted the windows.

"Room eleven has to be right there," he said, indicating the third window from the left. Luckily, the curtains weren't closed all the way.

"How are we going to see anything?" demanded Cora. "It's too high."

"No problem," said Max. He grabbed a nearby trash can and dragged it under the window. "This should work."

Ivy looked at the trash can and groaned. "But it stinks."

"Sorry, Ivy," said Max with a grin. "You want to help your dad, right?"

Ivy nodded. "Yeah."

"Then start climbing," Max said. "You're the lightest, so you get to be the lookout. Come on, I'll give you a boost."

Sid and Cora held the garbage can steady and Max hoisted Ivy up. Standing on the lid, Ivy's nose barely reached the bottom of Mr. Sherman's window.

"What do you see?" asked Max, gripping her legs so she didn't fall.

Ivy stood on her tiptoes. "Nothing," she whispered. "A bed and a suitcase."

"Maybe he left," suggested Sid.

"What are we going to do now?" cried

Cora. "I knew this was a dumb idea. Why did I listen to you, Max? All your ideas are dumb."

"Hey," said Max, insulted. "Do you want my help or not?"

Cora's shoulders slumped. "Yes."

"Fine," said Max. He turned back to Ivy. "He's got to be in there. When I called earlier, they rang me through to his room and he answered before I hung up."

"Wait," whispered Ivy. "I see him!"

"What's he doing?" asked Max.

"He just came out of the bathroom," reported Ivy. "And he's not using his crutches! Quick, pass me the camera."

Before Max could hand her the camera, Ivy let out a disappointed sigh.

"He went back into the bathroom," she said.

"How can we videotape him when he's hiding in the bathroom?" wailed Cora.

Max chewed his lip. They were running out of time. Just like a director who takes a scene in a different direction, Max had to change his plan.

"Time for a re-write," he decided. "If Mr. Sherman won't come out, then I'll have to go in."

12 ...With My Little Eye

"Are you crazy?" asked Sid. "You can't just waltz into his hotel room. What if he recognizes you from the bike shop?"

"He won't. He barely even looked at us," said Max. He tucked the camera out of sight and took a deep breath. "Keep watching the window," he instructed. "I'll be right back."

He strode over to the back exit door and tugged on the handle. He slipped inside and walked quickly through the halls, hoping no one would question his presence. Room eleven was easy to find. Max stopped outside the door, unsure what to do next.

A rattling noise made him spin around. A man in a white uniform pushed a breakfast cart down the hall toward Max. The dishes clanked together as he walked. The man stopped in front of room nine and knocked at the door, then looked at Max.

"Are you lost, kid?" he asked.

"Er, no," said Max. "I'm just waiting for my dad."

He leaned against the wall, trying to look bored. He hoped his acting was more convincing than Sid's.

The man knocked again. "Must be sleeping or something," he said with a shrug. He turned and walked away, leaving the cart outside the door.

As soon as he was out of sight, Max sprang into action. "Sweet dreams," he whispered to the door of room nine.

Working quickly, Max wheeled the breakfast cart over to room eleven and lifted the hem of the white tablecloth that covered it. Underneath was a stainless steel shelf. He slipped the camera onto the shelf, then let the tablecloth fall back into place.

Then Max slid a cloth napkin out from under some cutlery and draped it over his arm. He knocked briskly on the door.

"Room Service," he called out.

Muffled thumps and thuds reached Max's ears before the door opened and Mr. Sherman stuck his head into the hall. He wore a white robe and his face was covered in shaving cream.

"What?"

"Room Service," said Max again. He tried not to stare at the area above Mr. Sherman's upper lip. Even covered in shaving cream, Max could tell it was moustache-free.

"Must be some mistake," said Mr. Sherman, leaning on his crutches. "I didn't order anything."

Max gulped. "Compliments of the house," he blurted out. "It's, um, our anniversary."

Mr. Sherman smiled behind the shaving

cream. "Really? Well, then, come right in."

Max pushed the cart into the room with a silent sigh of relief. Just as the door shut behind him, he thought he heard another door in the hallway, possibly the one to room nine, open.

"Are you enjoying your stay at the Blackberry Inn?" asked Max. His gaze darted around the small room. If this were a film, he would just direct Mr. Sherman to watch television or something so he could stash the camera somewhere. But this was real life and Mr. Sherman sat on the edge of the bed, wiped the shaving cream off of his face with a towel, and picked up the serving tray lid.

"Yeah, sure," said Mr. Sherman. He grabbed a fork. "Mmmm, eggs. And French toast. Thanks, kid. This is great. You can let yourself out."

Max panicked. He couldn't leave the room yet! Thinking fast, Max held out his hand, palm up.

Mr. Sherman looked at him, then laughed. "Right. Almost forgot the tip. Hold on, my pants are in the bathroom."

He hobbled to the bathroom and Max spun into action. Dropping to his knees, he reached under the cart and grabbed the camera, then thrust it into a potted fern that sat on the dresser beside the television. He made sure the lens cap was off and adjusted a feathery frond to cover the blinking green light.

A loud crash came from the bathroom. "Rotten crutches," yelled Mr. Sherman.

"Are you okay in there?" called Max, jumping to his feet.

"Yeah, hold on," said Mr. Sherman. "I'll be right out."

Max spotted the clock radio bolted to the bedside table. Did he dare? More clanking noises came from the bathroom. It sounded like Mr. Sherman had dropped his crutches in the bathtub. Making up his mind, Max darted over to the radio and switched it on.

Flipping frantically, he located a lively station. The music sounded Mexican or something, like the stuff Mom played when she was taking Salsa dance lessons. He turned up the volume and darted back to his spot just as Mr. Sherman lurched out of the bathroom.

"Here you go," said Mr. Sherman. He

dropped a few coins into Max's hand, then cocked his head to one side, listening, a puzzled expression on his face.

"Thank you, sir," said Max, backing quickly toward the door.

A second later, he was hurrying down the hall. He edged past a couple in matching white bathrobes arguing with a hotel employee in the doorway of room nine. It took every ounce of willpower Max had to not break into a run. Then he was back in the alley.

"That was so brave, Max," said Ivy with an adoring smile.

Max felt his face go hot. He shrugged. "I just hope it works. He used the crutches when I was there, but now that he's alone, or thinks he's alone, there won't be any reason to pretend."

"He'd better do something fast," muttered Cora, looking at her watch. "Daddy is running out of time."

Max took Ivy's place on the trash can and carefully raised his head until he could see through the window.

"And . . . action," he whispered.

13 Caught in the Act

"What's he doing?" hissed Cora.

Max shushed her with one hand, holding onto the windowsill for balance with the other. He peered through the gap in the curtain. "He's eating," he whispered.

"That's not going to help Daddy," complained Cora.

"Wait," whispered Max. "He's . . . oh, never mind. He's still eating. Why did those people have to order such a big breakfast?"

"What people?" asked Sid, confused.

"I'll explain later," said Max. One of his sneakers slid on the trash can's rounded lid, and he gripped the windowsill tighter.

Ivy looked at her watch. "It's 9:30," she reported.

Max continued to stare through the window. His fingers were getting sore and his sneakers kept slipping on the slick metal. *Come on, Mr. Sherman,* he urged silently. *Do something!*

Then, just like an actor taking orders from a

director, Mr. Sherman took one last gulp of coffee, wiped his mouth on a napkin, and stood up. Without his crutches.

"Yes!" cried Max under his breath. He couldn't see the camera in the fern, but he knew it was there, recording everything. "Come on, now, take a few steps."

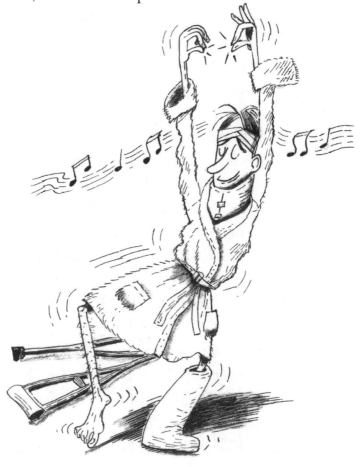

Mr. Sherman stood in one spot for what seemed like forever to Max, then cocked his head to one side as though he was listening to something. His chin bobbed. His fingers snapped. Then, right in front of Max and the hidden camera, he started to dance.

Max watched, open mouthed, as Mr. Sherman twirled and dipped and clapped his hands above his head in time to the lively Latin music. A few notes floated out to the alley. Max chuckled and watched Mr. Sherman spin around the room. Almost of their own accord, Max's toes begin to tap in time to the irresistible beat.

"Knock it off," whispered Sid, straining to hold the trash can steady.

"It's working!" Max grinned down at the girls. "My plan is actually working!"

"It's 9:45," said Ivy. She looked up at Max anxiously. "Um, don't you think we'd better go save Daddy now?"

"Right," said Max, bobbing with the beat. The trash can rocked with him. "We've got enough evidence on tape to put Mr. Sherman away for fraud and blackmail and probably a whole bunch of other things. All we have to do is get the camera and take it . . ."

"Watch out," cried Sid. She grabbed for the swaying trash can, but not fast enough.

"Ahhhhhh," cried Max, clutching the windowsill with both hands as the trash can shot out from under his feet. The lid hit the ground with an awful clatter. The can itself flew in the other direction, knocking Sid over and barreling into several other garbage cans. The noise echoed up and down the alley.

Max dangled from the window, his chin on the sill. Inside the hotel room, the music abruptly stopped. Mr. Sherman turned his head toward the window, looking straight into Max's startled eyes.

Max glanced below him and saw that the alley was empty. Sid and Cora and Ivy had vanished. He knew he had to jump and escape too, but he couldn't make his fingers release their grip. Not when recognition came into Mr. Sherman's eyes. Not when Mr. Sherman marched over to the window and jerked it open. Not even when he thrust his nose into Max's face, so close that Max could smell ketchup on his breath.

Then, before Max could say a word, Mr. Sherman grabbed him and hauled him into room eleven.

14 Fire Alarms and Fleeing Ferns

"What are you doing?" said Mr. Sherman in a low, threatening voice.

Max gulped. "Well, uh, you see . . ."

Mr. Sherman narrowed his eyes, and his grip on Max's shirt tightened. "I never forget a face," he said. "You're the room service kid."

Max gulped. "Did you enjoy your breakfast, sir?" he asked in a faint voice.

"I asked you a question," roared Mr. Sherman. "Why are you spying on me?"

When Max didn't answer, Mr. Sherman shoved him roughly onto the bed. "You know," he said, studying Max almost thoughtfully, "you seem awful young to be working at a hotel."

"I'm small for my age," said Max.

Mr. Sherman shook his head. "You look very familiar. I feel like I've seen you somewhere before..."

"I have one of those faces," Max told him.

"Wait!" he cried, staring at Max. "I remember where I saw you. It was at the bike shop. You were with those Thompson brats!"

"N–n–no," stammered Max.

Mr. Sherman ran his fingers through his hair until it stood on end. "This is worse than I thought," he muttered to himself. Charlotte is going to be furious." He paced the room, back and forth in front of the fern. "She's going to say I messed up just like last time. Well, I didn't! I'll take care of this situation myself. Charlotte doesn't ever have to know."

Max gulped. He didn't like the idea of being taken care of. He glanced at the window. It was still open, but it was much too far away. The door was closer. Unfortunately, Mr. Sherman stood between it and Max. No escape there, either.

Mr. Sherman seemed to have forgotten Max. He paced the floor, mumbling to himself. If this were a movie, Max would simply create a diversion with special effects. An unexpected thunderstorm and a bolt of lighting through the window. Or an earthquake that would throw Mr. Sherman to the floor and knock him unconscious. It was so easy in the movies. Real life was a bit trickier.

Suddenly an alarm went off. It blasted through the entire hotel, ringing so loud that it shook the walls. Startled, Mr. Sherman cried out, covering his ears with his hands. He yanked open the door and peered into the corridor where people were pouring out of their hotel rooms.

Max flew into action. First, he grabbed the crutches and fired them out the window. Then he snatched up the fern, pot and all, and dashed under Mr. Sherman's arm, out into the hallway. Glancing over his shoulder, he saw Mr. Sherman start to follow him, then stop. Just as Max had hoped, he couldn't give chase through a crowd of witnesses without his crutches or his moustache.

Max raced through the crowd. The alarm was deafening. Terrified shrieks pierced the loud ringing. Somewhere, a child screamed. Max kept on running.

Sid was waiting at the back exit. On the wall beside her was a fire alarm with the lever pulled down. Max flashed her a grateful grin and they both dashed through the door to the alley outside.

"To the bike shop!" gasped Max.

They raced down the alley and whipped around the corner onto Main Street. Ivy and Cora stood on the sidewalk outside the bike shop door. When Max and Sid came into sight, Ivy jumped up and down, waving her watch in the air.

"It's 9:59," she cried. "Hurry, Max, hurry!"

Cora held open the door and Max raced through it without slowing down. As he neared the office at the rear of the store, he saw Mr. Thompson hold a long, slender piece of paper out to Charlotte's crimson-tipped fingers.

"Nooooooo!" hollered Max. He hurtled forward, upsetting a display of bike helmets and sending a rack of reflector lights flying. Both Charlotte and Mr. Thompson turned toward him with surprised faces.

Max screeched to a stop directly in front of them. Clutching the fern in one hand, he reached out with the other and deftly snatched the check out of Charlotte's fingers.

"I'll take this," he said.

15 Max the Movie Man

"Hey!" cried Charlotte. "Give that back!"

Max glanced at the check. The line where you write in the amount was filled with lots and lots of zeros. Lovely, round zeros. Max looked at them longingly, then sighed and crumpled the check into a tight ball.

"What are you doing?" cried Charlotte. She stared at the ruined check, horrified. "That's mine!"

"Not anymore," said Max with a triumphant smile. Finally, something he was directing was going the way he wanted it to. Come to think of it, this would make a great mystery movie.

"I'm so sorry, Ms. Tann," said Mr. Thompson. He turned to Max. "I know you're probably trying to help, but we're conducting important business here. Now, would you please excuse us while I write out another check?"

"No, Daddy, don't!" cried Ivy. She ran to her

father and grabbed him by the arm. "She's trying to steal your money!"

"Ivy, please," said Mr. Thompson. "This is no time for . . ."

"It's true, Mr. Thompson," said Max. "It's all a big con. She's in cahoots with Mr. Sherman."

"That's preposterous!" exclaimed Charlotte. She glared at Max. "I don't have to listen to this nonsense. Mr. Thompson, do we or do we not have a deal?"

"No!" cried the children in unison.

Mr. Thompson shook his head, confused. "I don't understand."

"It's all true," said Max. "She really is a con artist. In fact, she tried the same thing over in Harrington last year. Call my dad and ask him."

"I'm losing my patience," said Charlotte. She snapped her briefcase shut and stood up. "Perhaps I made a mistake coming here. If you don't want to settle this now, Mr. Thompson, then we'll see you in court."

"Please, wait," said Mr. Thompson. He turned to Max. "You can't just come in here and throw accusations around like that. I'd like to believe you, but I don't know what to think, and I can't afford to get dragged into court. Unless you have some kind of evidence . . ."

Max thrust the fern into Mr. Thompson's arms. "Here you go."

Mr. Thompson stared at the bedraggled plant. "What's this?"

Max grinned. "Proof."

Charlotte took a step backward. "I've had enough. I'm leaving."

Cora blocked her way. "Aren't you going to stay for the show?" she asked.

Charlotte blinked at her suspiciously. "What are you talking about?"

Max parted the bruised and bent fern fronds and pulled out the camera. "Please, gather around. We're having a private showing," he said. "A Maximillian Productions original."

Max flipped open the camera's small viewing screen. "It's my first film," he explained. "I guess you could call it a musical. There's dancing in it. I was lucky enough to get a fairly well-known dancer to play the lead, a fellow named Sherman Windler. Perhaps you've heard of him?"

Charlotte froze. "No."

"Well, maybe you'll recognize his face," said Max. He rewound the tape, then pushed play.

On the tiny screen, surrounded by a hazy green frame, Mr. Sherman appeared, eating French toast and eggs. A small gasp escaped Charlotte's lips.

"Please bear with me," said Max. "I haven't had a chance to edit." He pushed fast-forward and Mr. Sherman forked eggs into his mouth like he was trying to win a speed-eating contest. He chugged his coffee, slapped his mouth with a napkin and leaped to his feet. Then, still in fast-forward, he whirled and jumped around the room like a ballerina on a sugar high. It looked for all the world like an old, silent movie.

"I've seen enough," said Charlotte quietly.

"But there's more, and it will be even better with sound," cried Max. "Mr. Sherman threatens to kill me, and your name comes up and then the fire alarm goes off . . ."

"Fire alarm?" repeated Mr. Thompson. He sank into his chair, dazed. "Death threats? Con artists?"

Ivy hugged him around the neck. "Don't

worry, Daddy. Max got it all on tape."

"That's right," said Max. "I have a feeling my movie is going to be a smash hit on the big screen – down at the police station."

16 The Final Scene

Max's movie *was* a smash hit with the Brooksville Police. There was enough evidence to put Charlotte Tann and her accomplice, Sherman Windler, aka Willy Sherman, in jail for a long, long time. Mr. Thompson's bike shop was safe, and Ivy and Cora gazed at Max like adoring groupies. Everything was back to normal.

"Why do you look so glum?" asked Sid the next day. She glanced around Max's backyard. The broken garden gnome had been removed, the daisies were straightened, and a large ball of tinfoil sat in a corner, abandoned.

Max lay on the grass and stared at the clouds. "I don't know," he said. "I guess I thought that making a movie was going to be my ticket to the big time. But it failed, just like all my other ideas."

"It didn't exactly fail," said Sid. "It got two bad people off the streets, and saved the bike shop."

"Yeah," agreed Max. "But nobody's exactly lining up to see it, are they?"

Just then Ivy raced around the corner of the Wigglesworth house with Cora right behind her. "Max! Max!" she cried. "We've got great news!"

Max sat up. "What is it?"

"It's your movie," gasped Ivy. Her face was beet red from running. "You're going to be famous after all!"

"What are you talking about?" asked Max. "The police have it."

"Yeah," said Cora. "But they let Daddy have a copy. He's showing it tonight at his Bike Safety Seminar!"

"Will you come?" asked Ivy.

"Of course!" exclaimed Max. He jumped to his feet, his eyes wide with excitement. "There might be a big-shot movie producer in the audience. Or a Hollywood talent scout, or something like that."

"In Brooksville?" asked Sid, raising a skeptical eyebrow.

Max didn't seem to hear her. "This could be

my big chance!" he cried. "Has anybody seen my tam?"

Sid laughed. "Come on, Mr. Director, I'll help you look."

That night, Max and Sid walked to the town hall together. The parking lot was jam-packed with cars. Someone had taped a sign on the front door saying, "FILM TONIGHT: MAX WIGGLESWORTH, DIRECTOR".

A delightful shiver crawled down Max's spine. He took a pair of Mom's oversized sunglasses out of his pocket and slipped them on.

"How do I look?" he asked.

Sid gave him the thumbs up sign. "Simply marvelous," she told him.

Max took a deep breath, adjusted his tam, then pushed open the door and walked inside. From behind the sunglasses, he surveyed the room. The audience was filled with familiar faces – kids from school, friends of his parents, even Officer Todd from the police station. At the front of the room stood Mr. Thompson, holding a microphone. Cora and Ivy stood nearby, grinning from ear to ear.

"Welcome, everyone, to this month's Bike Safety Seminar," Mr. Thompson announced. The chatter in the room faded away. "We're going to start the meeting with a movie. I'm pleased to say that we have the genius behind the camera, Max Wigglesworth, here with us tonight."

There was a smattering of applause. Max pushed the sunglasses to the top of his head and gave the audience a jaunty salute. There were a few smothered giggles, which quickly turned to coughs.

The lights dimmed and a large screen at the front of the room lit up. Max and Sid squeezed into two seats in the back row. At first everything was blurry. Then Max's sneaker came into focus, followed by an extreme close-up of several blades of grass.

A few more giggles rose from the audience.

"I must have forgotten it was on," whispered Max. "Don't worry, I'll edit that out in post-production."

Suddenly, the camera swung up and Sid's

face filled the screen. It was so large that her nostrils were the size of dinner plates. Sid slouched in her seat as the giggles increased.

The next ten minutes were a blur of Sid wobbling, tripping, falling, crashing, and half killing herself on her bike. The audience chuckled when she got tangled in the garden hose. They chortled when she ran over the garden gnome, and they roared with laughter when she landed in the dirt pile.

When the movie ended, Mr. Thompson put the lights back on. "Who can tell me which bike safety rules were broken in this film?"

Hands shot up all over the room.

"Always wear a helmet!" cried a boy.

"Wear suitable clothing!" shouted someone else.

"Watch where you're going!"

"Keep both hands on the handlebars!"

"This is humiliating," whispered Sid. She slouched low in her seat. "Let's get out of here."

"Hold on," said Max. He stared at Mr. Thompson, striding back and forth on stage, pointing at people and shouting into his microphone. He reminded Max of someone. An auctioneer, maybe, selling items to the highest bidder.

The gears in Max's brain started to click. Perhaps getting rich by making a movie was a little far-fetched after all. Too many middlemen, anyway. Publicists and agents and marketing executives, all taking a piece of the pie.

Max shook his head. He needed get his hands on the money directly. Being an auctioneer wasn't a bad idea, really. People loved to buy dusty old stuff. Antiques, Max corrected himself. Why, just last week he heard about a lady who'd found an ancient, stained painting in her attic and had sold it for three million dollars.

"Max!" Sid elbowed him in the ribs. "This meeting is going to last for another hour. Wanna sneak out?"

"Uh huh," said Max, ideas spinning in his head so fast he could hardly keep track of them.

Everyone he knew had junk stashed away in their attics or basements. Why, Mom and Dad had boxes of stuff collecting cobwebs in the garage right this minute. Most of it was worthless, but some of it had been handed down by Max's grandfather, Maximillian I. Who knows, maybe there was a valuable heirloom in there somewhere, just waiting for someone to find it.

"I'm going," declared Sid, "Before they play the movie again."

"Wait for me," said Max. He followed her outside, leaving the hum of voices behind them. If he didn't find anything in the garage, there was always Sid's attic. Or, better yet, they could spend their weekends going to flea markets and garage sales. Who knew what marvelous treasures were hidden under years of grime and filth?

Once they found a priceless antique, they would simply need to clean it up a bit. Then they'd have to put it in some fancy art auction, and . . .

"You're awfully quiet," said Sid. She stared at him through narrowed eyes. "You're not dreaming up another movie plot, are you?"

"Oh, don't worry, I'm out of show biz for

good," Max assured her. He walked for a few moments, then turned to her with a grin. "By the way, you're not allergic to dust, are you?"

Don't miss these other great adventures in the MAX-A-MILLION series:

Max the Magnificent
by Trina Wiebe

ISBN 1-894222-55-5 • $6.95 CDN • $5.95 US

More than anything in the world Max wants to be a millionaire, but so far all of his get-rich-quick schemes have been spectacular failures. Now he's come up with the perfect plan. With the help of his best friend Sid, Max goes undercover in the world of magic to discover the one secret that will lead him to riches. But magic is an illusion that can hide unpleasant surprises. Before long Max realizes there are more important things than being a millionaire.

NEW for Spring 2003

Max the Mighty Superhero
by Trina Wiebe

ISBN 1-894222-68-7 • $6.95 CDN • $5.95 US

"All superheroes do good deeds," says Max. "That makes people happy. And when people are happy, they give rewards. Sometimes big rewards."

Max is back with another "fool-proof plan" to become a self-made millionaire. All he and his sidekick, Sid, have to do is rescue a few kidnapped babies, save some lives, and the reward money will roll in. But things go haywire when the only baby they rescue has four feet and the owner has plenty to hide.